Winner of the 2nd International Three-Day Novel-Writing Contest . . .

Doctor Tin

Tom Walmsley

PULP PRESS
VANCOUVER

Also by Tom Walmsley:
Rabies
The Workingman
Lexington Hero
The Jones Boy
Something Red

DOCTOR TIN
COPYRIGHT © 1979 TOM WALMSLEY

SECOND PRINTING 1981

ISBN 0-88978-049-8

THIS IS A PULP BOOK
PUBLISHED BY PULP PRESS
P.O. BOX 3868
VANCOUVER CANADA
V7X 1A6

PRINTED AND BOUND IN CANADA

For Michiko

"I will arise and dust..."
—Jean-Paul Cortane

I

It would always remind McGraw of a late-night news broadcast, or a series of stills from a cheap detective magazine, and it did that night. The bright lights that made the riverbank, mud, pebbles, weeds into a large black and white documentary, the woman's legs insanely white against the mud, the rest of her body invisible—*when you die you become garbage.*

He had always thought that, too—corpses with the look of having been discarded by their owners, bearing no lustre, like secondhand clothes, dull, tired, finished. But nothing was as prominent in his mind at that moment as the fact that he would have to walk through the mud to reach her, and his shoes had set him back forty bucks.

"Davis, god damn it, I swear to Christ I'm getting a pair of fucking gumboots, maybe some coveralls, too. Look at this stuff," McGraw said.

"They got their pictures. Let's get into it," Davis said.

There was a wind from the north that had little to whip up on the bank. Something was making a funny, snapping sound with every gust. They were right on top of the body before they saw it had a garbage bag tied around it.

11

"Those are woman's legs, it's a woman," McGraw said.

"Why the hell do they do that stuff with the garbage bags?" Davis asked no one.

The big lights jerked around the area, never far from the target, and McGraw wished, just once, to find a body at, oh, two in the afternoon, say, a Wednesday afternoon on a downtown street. But he'd done that. The only difference was it didn't make him want to buy gumboots.

There was a woman inside the bag. Her hands were tied behind her back and her body was nude. She was wearing too much makeup and it had spread over her face, red and black. There was one large hoop earring still hooked in her right ear lobe.

"What are those things on her? Burns?"

They turned the body not quite over.

"Jesus Christ."

"Somebody hated her," Davis said. "Sick cocksucker."

"Listen, is that just the wind, or is it fucking raining?"

"Rain."

"Perfect," McGraw said. "Fucking perfect."

There were a half-dozen patrolmen watching, looking under-aged and useless. McGraw could tell just which ones were going to start vomiting.

"Simple enough," Davis said. "Must have driven up, dumped her and missed the water. The guy was scared and in a hurry. The other thing, does her face

12

ring any bells for you? I think I've seen her around."

"The vice boys, maybe?"

"Yeah, let's do that," Davis said. "Get the boys to take a peek. Let's do it right now."

"Let's get the fuck out of the rain," McGraw said. His shoes had had it.

The nightclerk was well-built but getting soft in the belly. He watched, as A.J. walked across the carpet toward him, with what he hoped was a cold look, actually turning his back—as A.J. reached the desk—to show the impossibility of their being business to transact.

"Hi, there," A.J. said. "I'd like room 1619 buzzed, okay?"

The clerk turned slowly to look at him. He'd decided on the Lee Marvin approach.

"Are you the one who's been phoning for that room? There is no one registered in 1619."

"How about somebody not registered?" A.J. said. "I know it's the right room number, she doesn't make those mistakes. Just like I know this is the hotel, all right? Give 'em a buzz."

"Would you like me to personally escort you out of the building?" the clerk said. His chest expanded as he spoke. Or maybe that was the wrong thing to do. It's all in the eyes and tone of voice.

A.J. showed him the gun.

13

"Would you like me to shove this up your ass and blow your cock off, you dumb shit?"

The clerk wasn't sure what was called for: a laugh, a sneer, or the actual disarming of A.J. He felt as though he'd just been clipped across the back of the knees.

"You'd better put that away." His voice came out in a whisper.

"Get the fucking key and let's get moving," A.J. said. "Push any buttons or any of that cute shit and keep in mind who gets it first, all right? Now let's go. I'm in a hell of a hurry."

To the clerk, as he unhooked the key from the board, it was all absurd déja vu. The dialogue sounded corny and he was somehow embarrassed. His mind watched the scene calmly, but confused, while his body insisted on acting out a series of movie clichés, his mouth uttered banalities, and he decided to carry on with at least some sense of style. That was until A.J. broke his hand with the gun as he pushed open the desk gate and he heard himself scream.

"Just to get us off on the right foot," A.J. said.

They crossed the lobby to the elevators, and A.J. steered the clerk toward the stairs. The pain from the broken hand was terrible and the clerk found he had no control over his body, which had begun to shake. His mouth was very dry, just like he'd read about. *It's no use how brave you are in your mind, if your body won't act brave,* he thought. It would take him

14

almost a year to forget this thought and re-establish his enthusiasm for *Point Blank*.

Room 1619, on the first floor, there being no rooms on the ground floor, was empty. The twin beds were made up and the ashtrays were clean.

"All right," A.J. said. "They were here and now they're not here anymore. Look at those fucking beds, guys made those beds, it doesn't fool me, you understand? Now what you're gonna tell me is who rented the fucking room and where I can find him, all right? It's that simple."

The clerk knew, as A.J. took a straight razor from his pocket with his free hand, that the hundred dollar bill Mr. Peterson had given him was not enough money to keep him from telling A.J. everything. Not nearly enough.

A.J. smiled.

McGraw sat at his kitchen table, waiting for the coffee. It looked wet and gray through the window, impossible to judge the time of day. In an apartment below, someone was banging the hell out of something metal with a hammer.

"What time is it?" McGraw said.

"Three hours later than when you went to bed. Harry, what in God's name happened to your shoes?"

15

His wife brought the coffee pot to the table and poured him a cup. She whitened and sweetened it herself. McGraw knew there was something dangerously wrong with a cop who used milk and sugar, but he couldn't get past it.

"Woman was killed and dumped near the river. Place was full of fucking mud."

"Couldn't they just bring the body to you?"

"No."

He picked up the cup and wondered how it would feel, losing a finger. Not too good, probably. If the thing was sharp enough and it happened fast enough, maybe you'd hardly feel it. People say that.

"She was a hooker. Some guy, or more likely a couple guys, killed her. She was covered in welts and burns, all sorts of stuff. Davis is just going to kill those fucking guys."

His wife had poured half a cup of coffee for herself, and halted in mid-pour.

"What kind of welts? Where? What kind of burns?" she asked.

"You don't want to hear about it."

"Was she naked? Tied up? Did they use a ..." her voice turned husky, "...a whip?"

"Doris, the fuck is wrong with you?"

Doris moved away from the table, replacing the pot on the stove.

"Can't I show a little interest in your work?" she said.

"Anyhow," McGraw went on, "the vice boys

16

made her. She's been around maybe a year, same address. We show up at the place, high-rise, and I want to tell you, it's quite a set-up. Whoever the bastard is she lived with is some character. Handcuffs, chains, leather masks, everything. Each corner of the bed had a little leather thing for holding down your hands and feet. Couldn't believe it. Is this making you upset?"

"No, no, go ahead," Doris said, sitting down.

"You looked a little funny there, for a second. Anyway, I guess she was a little nuts herself, going along with it. We figured the set-up was maybe for her tricks, but there's definitely a guy living there. Still, could be for tricks, if you had a bodyguard around, make sure you didn't get killed. So it's one of two things: trick works out on her and it gets out of hand, or her boyfriend."

"Was she...beaten...*to death?*

"No, no. Stabbed, just once. Stopped bleeding a long time before she got dumped. Hell of a thing. Now this apartment where she lived, the other weird thing, no T.V., no radio, no books, magazines, nothing, like she'd just moved in. But she'd been there a year, all her clothes are there, groceries, coffee, everything. In the whole place, all there was was a guitar and a writing pad by the phone. Nothing written in it, but you could see something was written on the first sheet and torn off. Davis ran a pencil over it, colouring it in..."

"Harry, that's so *old.*"

"Yeah, Davis said he hated to do it, but we had no choice. It was a room number, that's all. Called every hotel in town. Turns out, down at the Royal, the nightclerk's been worked over and dumped in a room. Guess which room? So..."

"You say...worked over...?"

"Somebody cut off one of his fingers. They sewed the finger back on, down at the hospital, but the guy was still out when we got there. I'm meeting Davis down there in—what?— half an hour, I guess. Try and find out what the fuck is going on."

"Do you want another coffee before you go?"

"Sure, that'd be fine." He watched his wife as she poured the coffee and replaced the pot.

"Listen, Doris," McGraw said, "does this stuff make you feel kind of—well—kind of *funny?*"

"Funny *how*, Harry?" Doris hissed. "Funny *how?*"

They stared across the table at each other, hearts pounding loudly, and McGraw felt he was at the beginning of a very interesting case, indeed.

Davis hadn't gone home at all. He'd had twelve cups of coffee from the vending machine in the hospital's waiting room and had urinated seventeen times. By the time the clerk struggled up from under the anaesthetic, Davis knew his first name was

Russell, he'd worked at the hotel four months, and his co-workers considered him an asshole.

The first thing Russell saw as the room came into focus was Davis taking his eighteenth piss in the jug beside the bed and a flash of white as the nurse fled the premises.

"Let's get down to it, Russell," Davis said. "Some jerk-off chopped off one of your pinkies and I'm going to find the guy and kick his fucking teeth out and break both his arms. Are you reading me, kid?"

Russell tried to scream, but all that came out was "Nurse" in a thick croak.

Davis grabbed the kid's jaw in his hand and pried the water jug between his teeth, drenching the pillow and sheets with fresh urine.

"Shit," said Davis.

"Nurse," Russell croaked.

Davis leapt to the sink, filled a paper cup, sprang back and forced the contents down the patient's throat.

"Now, talk," he told him.

"Nurse!" Russell screamed. He began to cry.

The head nurse and three members of the staff, accompanied by an oversized orderly, burst into the room.

All hell broke loose.

Mr. Peterson, despite the harrowing ordeal of the

night before, looked immaculate. He had slept badly, but it served only to give his face a stern and concerned cast. A man in his position should *always* appear somewhat stern and concerned.

He had only orange juice for breakfast, believing coffee to be essentially poisonous and breakfast an investment with little return. Mr. Peterson played handball three times a week, did not touch tobacco and drank alcohol only on occasion. On those occasions he turned into a wild beast, suffered blackouts, picked fights, spat, and removed his clothes in public places. Until last night he hadn't had a drink in six months, and certainly never drank in town. A long week-end in a small town some three hundred miles from his wife and family had always suited him and them, until last January, when he had arrived at the train station wearing one shoe and no socks, having lost the Buick on a bet, the premise of which forever remained obscure. A combination of candy, Valium, and iron will had kept him on the wagon. Until last night. At that time he and a couple of the boys drank twenty rounds of bourbon, tortured and murdered a prostitute, then dumped the body in the river.

"I'm abstaining for good," Mr. Peterson announced to himself in the mirror, removing a speck of lint from his lapel. He mused over the fact that a man could walk on the moon, but lint couldn't be conquered. What was lint, exactly? One of those things, like dust, that one takes for granted without ever fully investigating the facts.

He removed a small, leather-bound notebook from his inside pocket, a notebook too slender to bulge, and removed the cap from a silver-plated pen attached to the book's spine by a thin and equally silver chain. Opening the book to a clean page, he wrote in precise penmanship: *Investigate the Facts.*

He did not know, as he tiptoed quietly down the pine-scented hallway, that his wife, in her own bedroom, was not stirring restlessly and somewhat violently from the bad dreams that so frequently awakened her, but was being quickly and violently strangled to death by A.J., on her stomach, her face mashed into a pillow.

He did not know, as he stood outside her door, debating whether to peek in or simply leave for work, that A.J. stood only a foot on the other side, eyes on fire, breathing quietly through his dirty teeth, his ears filled with the roaring of his own blood.

When the situation gets too extreme down at headquarters, when key witnesses are in the bowels of schizophrenic attack, when too many nerves are stretched and sing like high-tension wires, on the large scale or the small, they send in Max. Max can send out calm with a warm, dry force that puts hysterics on the nod. He radiates peace the way A.J. radiates violence, and today radios crackle and

21

phones go dead in A.J.'s wake. If Max and A.J. come within ten yards of each other they are apt to fuse and explode, leaving only a huge tear in time, a great yawn of anti-matter in the hospital corridor that will chew up everything and spit out nothing, including Davis' and McGraw's case.

But this isn't likely—no-one wants Max around long. He has the Great Calm, a soft blue aura, but nothing else, an idiot with no deductive or organizational abilities and a bore. His only contact with police work is a time like this, when a man has not only a broken hand but a finger removed from that hand, and has awakened to a mouthful of warm piss. Max is in the room, getting the story, alone, cooling the victim out.

"I thought I was giving him water," Davis snarled in the corridor. "They should label those fucking jugs."

The headquarters P.R. man, having spent the better part of two hours placating innumerable injured parties, lost patience for the first time.

"Davis," the P.R. man growled, "you are a god damned animal and owe your badge to the fact that the chief is out of town. Now, slow down."

Their eyes met in silent, intent fury, a long pause until the P.R. man spoke, his mouth growing soft.

"But you're a hell of a cop and we could use a hundred more like you."

Davis' eyes misted. He looked at his hands and mumbled. The P.R. man dropped his head, cleared

22

his throat, and left. McGraw kicked mud from his shoes under the baleful and moronic gaze of an orderly.

Then, of a sudden, a feeling of twilight infected the hallway, bringing vague but comforting memories of a pair of brown shoes you wore when you were six, strange phrases coming to the lips, names of pets from years ago: Max approaches.

After months of hit-and-miss, the department discovered the only way to receive a report from Max was via tape recorder. But when the news must be transferred immediately, there are only two alternatives: by telephones separated by a suitable distance, or in an open space, screaming at the top of your lungs to ensure concentration. If you have no questions, scream periodically anyway, to keep on your toes. The telephones in the hospital waiting area were separated by no more than six feet. Davis, Max and McGraw headed for the exits at a dead run.

"WHO CUT HIS FINGER OFF?" Davis bellowed, a dozen feet away on the lawn of the hospital's east wing.

"WHAT WAS GOING ON IN ROOM 1619?" shouted McGraw.

"Fellows, it's like this," spoke Max in his remarkable baritone, which contained the insinuation not only of the Pacific, but triggered memories of Gregorian chant, "this boy is a nice boy, but a bit of an asshole. A Mr. Peterson, whom the lad has dealt with before, and whose business card I now hold in my hand, rented room 1619 last night about eight, with two other gentlemen. They went out about nine and returned with a young woman whose description fits that…''

"AAAAAAHHHH!" shouted Davis.

"WOOOOOOOOO!" went McGraw.

''. . . of the deceased. Approximately ninety minutes later, Mr. Peterson approached the boy and explained that the girl was drunk and had passed out and they had discovered she was under-age, though Russell thought this hardly the case.''

"McGRAW, GRAB THE FUCKING BUSINESS CARD! MOVE IN ON HIM FAST!" Davis shrieked.

McGraw darted in, snatched up the card, but slowed to a dog-trot, returning.

"KEEP RUNNING TILL YOU REACH THE CAR!" Davis directed. "MAX, WRAP IT UP!"

"In any case, Russell kept watch for the men while they took the girl out the back way, wrapped in their coats. Mr. Peterson gave him a one hundred dollar bill to keep quiet about the incident. He claims all three of the men were intoxicated.'' Max smiled in contentment.

"THE FINGER! THE FUCK HAPPENED TO HIS FINGER?"

"At this point, the boy is vague about time. It was after midnight, perhaps after one. He has suffered a severe shock, Davis.''

"Aaaaahhhhh," spoke Davis.

"You're drifting, I'll make this brief: male, dark

24

hair, in need of a shave, about 5'10", 160, showed up at the desk, forced Russell to take him to the room at gunpoint after pistol-whipping him, then cut off his finger with a straight razor. Cuts first, asks questions later. The kid gave him Peterson's name and home address.''

"HOW'D HE KNOW IT? WHAT IS IT?''

"Mr. Peterson frequented the hotel. Always used the same address, apparently his own, on the register. Must have kept things straight for tax deduction. Can you imagine doing that? What if his wife discovered it? Of course, he may have told her...''

"THE FUCKING ADDRESS!''

"One-eleven Riverend Road. Distinctive, in a way...''

But Davis was sprinting for the car.

Mel and Jack, both good boys and true, many miles from their respective homes on separate business trips but friends of long standing, tossed together by happy coincidence, walked into the hotel bar. They had been separated all day by business that couldn't wait and it had been a nervous day, indeed. At noon, Mel had picked up a newspaper and found a vague mention of the hooker's death that left him feeling precisely as nervous as he was before obtaining the paper. But the late edition carried

25

tidings of the untimely demise of Peterson and his wife. The paper failed to connect the "shocking and horrifying" deaths of the Petersons in their chic bungalow with the mere "slaying" of a prostitute left in the mud near a river that would never support life, but Mel and Jack had what could be called the straight goods. It was news enough to totally unstring Mel, but Jack was calmer, as he had always been.

As Jack so levelheadedly pointed out, there might be no connection whatsoever between the two incidents. How would anyone know where she was, let alone who she was with?

Because she was a careful girl, she used the john downstairs before we even went up to the room, is there a phone in that john? Why did she want the room number to begin with, why did we give her the right one, would she have thrown a screaming fit if the numbers didn't tally? Who did she phone?
—but Mel knew he was being paranoid.

Furthermore, Jack said, being hardheaded and realistic about the whole thing, it was better for them that Peterson was dead. However cold it sounded, Peterson was the only link between them and the girl. The kid at the desk, if they ever got that far (which they wouldn't) could describe two average-looking guys who wouldn't be in town by the end of the week.

This was a fine theory and made Mel feel as good as he could under the circumstances, until two things happened. The first was the mention over the radio of the nightclerk losing a finger at the Royal, an item so buried in the papers it had been missed by both of them. This piece of information sent them downstairs for a drink. It was on their way into the bar that the second thing happened.

"Did your friend get ahold of you?" the bartender asked them.

"What friend's that?"

"Fellow came in about, oh, couple of hours ago, just asked if Mel and Jack had been in yet. I told him you weren't generally in the bar that early and to ask at the desk. I guess he didn't."

The bartender didn't tell them what unheralded visions sprang across the back of his eyes when he had looked up and seen A.J., large splashes of red decorating the mind's scenery, making him sit down, short of breath and fearsome of blood pressure. Instead, he described A.J. as best he could, trying not to be unflattering as it was a friend, then brought them their drinks.

"Holy good Jesus fucking bloody shit," said Mel, after taking one huge gulp of bourbon.

"It's simple," Jack said, forever the calmer. "We sleep in my room tonight, we don't let anyone in. They won't let the bastard past the desk at this place, by the sound of him. In the morning we get the fuck out of here, get a place on the other side of town. The cops'll get him before he ever gets us. I've got business to do in this town."

Mel seemed a little less tense as he downed his

drink and in that moment, the light from the bar glinting, as light will, through the thick bottom and sides of Mel's glass, Jack felt fear as he had never known it before grip the back of his neck in a dull, dead hand, felt his bowels loosen and his sweat glands do what they're known for. That was no kind of fucking plan at all.

"The thing that pisses me off," Mel said, "is with Peterson. Family man, hell of a good guy, big position downtown, and some god damned pimp cuts him up over a whore."

"Shut up," Jack said, thick-tongued. "I'm trying to think."

It was dark enough to turn a light on, but Davis didn't turn on any lights. He was supposed to be getting a couple of hours sleep, but Davis wasn't thinking about sleeping. He sat looking at the darkening wall, a spring so tight that one more turn will make sure the clock never runs again. Davis has interrupted radio reception himself, this day.

—I got to get this fucking guy, is all he can think. Now, you got a whore dead, dead in a bad way, I'm as pissed off as anyone about it. But this guy, the way he's acting is, is—what is it?—*out of proportion.* (A phrase Davis has heard more than twice).

The guys who killed that girl—Peterson and who-

28

ever—they shouldn't have done it, things got out of hand for sure, but *this fucking guy*. Now this guy is a real menace. Say a guy, well, okay, a guy breaks into your apartment, rips off the T.V. Do you track him down and blow his head off? You call the law. This isn't the same as that, though. All right, all right, so a guy feels up your little kid—true, you probably belt him a couple times but you wouldn't wipe out his family, would you?

Davis doesn't know what he's getting at, but he's trying to get at *something*. There is the awful memory of Peterson with his ears hacked off, thumbs removed and amputated penis and scrotum, apparently in that order, fresh in his mind.

—Now you can't tell me any guy deserves that, no matter what he did—Davis can agree with himself on this point.

—What about his wife, what'd she do to hurt anybody? Now the difference is, this hooker, the fuck was her name, she *liked* all that stuff. True, she probably didn't like getting killed but, god damn it, that's why you got cops. Also, what if these guys didn't do it to her? Like, what if her boyfriend worked her over first, she goes to turn the trick, tries to rip the guys off, maybe pulls a knife on them and gets stabbed in the fight? That's been known to happen. That's probably even what *did* happen and the guys got scared.

The entire day has been spent running down every single acquaintance of Peterson's, none of whom

29

went out with him the night before. Where did Peterson usually drink? Three hundred miles out of town.

—Who the fuck are those other guys? Find them, I'll get the son of a bitch. I got to get this guy. A guy like him around makes everything...like, if people can act like that, what you got on your hands...shit.

There is a word, but Davis can't think what it is.

McGraw was tired, after a hell of a long day of making the rounds of every likely-seeming bar showing people a company photograph of Peterson, dozens of people to track down and question, and all those tedious things that make a cop's life no bowl of cherries, brutalize him, etc. He went home for dinner feeling underpaid and unappreciated by the community at large. The discovery of Peterson's body had not made his day, either, and he decided to omit the gory details when relating it to Doris who, even now, was expecting him home—and a great little cook she was, too. As he trudged through the door of their apartment, it would be fair to say McGraw was taking the bitter with the sweet.

The first thing he saw was Doris's legs, bare, lying across the threshold of the bathroom. Her upper body was covered in a green garbage bag. McGraw, not breathing, not thinking—in fact, some distance from his own body, watching his actions—fell down beside his wife and tore the bag away, not recognizing his own hands as he did so. Her hands were handcuffed behind her back and her buttocks had a smattering of tiny burns. She was quite nude.

Still not breathing, thinking only enough to recognize the handcuffs as a pair of his own, McGraw turned the body over and looked into the face of his wife, tears welling out of her adorable blue eyes.

"Oh, Harry," Doris sobbed, "it isn't fun *at all!*"

McGraw fumbled up the key that was lying between his wife's nifty legs and unlocked the cuffs, as one would expect, expertly. His hands were shaking. Even with milk, he was drinking too much coffee.

"For God's sake, Doris," McGraw croaked.

"I did it for us, darling," said Doris, wrapping her arms around her husband. "I even burned myself with a cigarette and it *hurt!*"

She pulled back suddenly and looked at McGraw's face, the birth of delight in her cute, pixie features.

"Harry! I didn't like it!" she squealed. "Do you know what that means? *I'm normal!*"

Their mouths met, saliva mixing like lava, and they rolled on the bathroom tiles imprisoned by the claws of a greater passion than they ever knew existed.

The phone began to ring.

By the time the bar closed, Jack had covered all the possibilities and come up with nothing. They could change hotels, but sure as hell the bastard was somewhere close by, watching. Neither he nor Mel had gone to the washroom unaccompanied all evening.

They could go to a different hotel and be followed and killed there. They could tell the police their lives had been threatened, throwing far too harsh a spotlight on themselves. Going to them with the truth was unthinkable, as was being arrested for the security of a jail cell—what would the mother company make of that? Neither one of them could possibly leave town at that moment, not without ending their lives as men of business, and both men would have been hard pressed trying to draw any distinction between business life and breathing life.

Jack knew Mel was drunk because he was wearing an assertive, in fact, aggressive sneer that graced his face at no other time. Mel knew Jack was drunk because he, Mel, was good and fucking drunk and he'd like to see the day he couldn't drink that bastard under the place people are always drinking each other. They had matched each other drink for drink all night.

"All right," Mel said. "We go to the fucking room, jam the fucking bed against the door, get some shut-eye. Right? Tomorrow we take it from there. Right? Good fucking plan."

"My plan, don't forget, my plan," said Jack. "Mine."

And it sounded like a good fucking plan, all of a sudden.

This place was somewhat classier than the last one, and A.J. had anticipated trouble. He could see he was going to get some. There was one man behind the desk talking to another man in a uniform, some type of security officer who wore no sidearm. There was a bellboy, at that absurd hour, and some jerk in a suit.

The suit approached him when he was eight feet through the door.

"Can I help you, sir?"

The two men at the desk looked at A.J. with incurious expressions that changed rapidly as he sidestepped the man in front of him and continued walking. Behind him, A.J. heard the suit snap his fingers and saw the bellboy jump up and approach him from his right. The security guard stepped away from the desk and took two very masculine, very adult steps toward him. The clerk moved over to the telephone.

A.J. showed them the gun.

"Keep away from that fucking telephone or..."

He couldn't finish. Threats were beneath him.

The two men by the desk halted all movement immediately. A.J. took a quick, sideways step, turning and swinging the gun toward the bellhop and the suit.

"Get over by the desk, junior. You, too, fuck-face."

Uncertainly at first, then carefully, the bellboy and fuckface walked over to the desk.

"This is a bad mistake you're making, son," the security man said.

A.J. assumed it was the line he was paid to say, and let it go. He had learned one great thing that day, and it was something he'd always suspected: you need fear nothing, and be stopped by nothing, if you are prepared to use any amount of violence to fulfill an ambition. Having to hold four men at bay when he was on his way to kill two more didn't bother A.J.

"You got two guys staying here," he told the clerk. "One's called Mel, one's Jack. Find the rooms."

"We register by last names," said the clerk. "Sir."

"I'll settle for an M and a J," A.J. said. "These boys are probably a couple of high rollers—nobody here heard of good old Mel and Jack?"

"This is ridiculous," fuckface said, looking impatient and almost bored.

The way they look when you ask them anything, A.J. thought. Ask them a simple question, even. Or try and tell them a funny story. It has been a long time since A.J. told anyone a funny story.

"Tony," fuckface continued, "give him whatever cash we have on hand, and he can be on his way."

A.J. backhanded him with the gun across his

upper lip, brought the gun back against the side of his face, and clubbed him in the temple as he fell. The man in the suit gave two screams of shock and pain, then nothing with the third blow. A.J. swung the gun back to cover the other three, stepped in, and booted the fallen man in the side. Ribs snapped.

"Come to think of it," the security man said, "there were a couple of fellas asked me to keep an eye on things tonight. Went to the same room, 5201."

He looked embarrassed and afraid.

"Let's everybody get on the elevator," A.J. said. "You'll have to carry this guy."

Davis' idea had been this: if Peterson wasn't a local drinker, and the whereabouts of all his friends was accounted for, wasn't it possible he'd gone out on his own and struck up a friendship with a couple of guys while he was making the rounds? Likely he wouldn't even remember their last names. If he even remembered their *first* names, whoever cut his cock off knew those names. And that guy would go ask the bartender, at whatever bar they'd met at, to point them out.

With men out hunting up bartenders to show them a poor likeness of Peterson, Davis, catching McGraw at the inception of what promised to be the lay of his life,

35

sent him off to cover half the downtown bars, the kind of bars that Peterson would most likely stop at, and instructed him to ask the bartenders this question: did a guy—say a kind of weird guy who didn't look like he belonged in the place—come in and ask about a couple of guys? People ask about other people at bars, it's true, but Davis was counting on some bartender's intuition.

Only Davis would have come up with a plan that would entail such a tedious recounting. And come up with a man who remembered a red flash.

They had been parked across the road from the hotel, able to look into the lobby, for almost two hours when A.J. walked in. Up until that moment—in fact, until the moment they saw the gun—there was no saying that a guy asking after two other guys in a bar meant anything at all. Certainly not enough to ask for back-up, and scarcely enough to keep McGraw in the car.

To the immense satisfaction of Davis, they saw A.J. herding the four men near the counter at gunpoint.

"Let's do it," Davis said.

McGraw grabbed his arm and just as quickly dropped it. The two men stared at each other, neither one quite being able to believe the act.

"You *grabbed* me?" said Davis, wonderingly.

"What I mean is," said McGraw, "what if this is just a hold-up? We can take him on the way out. I don't want to end up with a hostage situation, here.''

"You fucking *grabbed* me?''

"I didn't mean to,'' McGraw said.

"You shoved your fucking meathook over here and wrapped your pinkies *around my sleeve,*'' Davis said. Saliva was forming near the corners of his mouth. "What *did* you mean?''

Just then McGraw saw A.J. clubbing the man in the suit.

"Look over there,'' McGraw said. "*Action.*''

Davis immediately snapped his head a hundred and eighty degrees in time to not only see A.J. in the act of pistol-whipping, but putting the boots to his victim.

"That's good enough for me,'' said Davis. He started out of the car.

"How do you want to handle this?'' McGraw asked, a pint nervously.

"Go right in and shoot the cocksucker,'' Davis said. "And don't fucking *touch* me.''

One look at the nightclerk's face, staring past him in disbelief, and A.J. knew it was all over. He gave his body a half-turn, snapping his arm out full length, and blew the glass out of the entrance door, sending Davis and McGraw to the pavement on their

37

bellies. His hostages scattered, hitting the deck, while he took off immediately, running in a crouch across the lobby toward the doorway marked STAIRS.

Davis' oversized handgun boomed three times as he crashed into the lobby, the first shot tearing a fist-sized chunk out of the doorjamb, the next two ripping off the doorknob and adding a huge, jagged period to STAIRS. But A.J. was already in the stairwell.

All McGraw could think, as they pounded across the carpeting, was: *this is for real.*

Racing up the first flight, his mind full of roaring, A.J. heard one of the cops screaming for the room number. Shit. Would they try and outrace him by elevator? No, a stupid move, trapped in a box when the doors opened to a jaundice-tinted overhead light flashing off A.J.'s wild eyes—no, they would come up right behind him. Or one would, and the other take the elevator, or more likely, the other stairway—were there two sets of stairs? Must be.

He had just turned the corner for the second floor when he heard the downstairs door loudly booted open, the cautious pause until the man below heard A.J.'s boots banging upwards, and the race began.

The kid probably had twenty years on him, Davis decided, and he wasn't likely to catch him on the stairs. Hugging the wall away from the handrail, eyes ever upward, running as best he could, Davis began firing at the blank wall at the top of every flight, two small flights per floor, hoping to catch the kid with a ricochet or scare him out of the whole project, even. Ears peeled for the sound of A.J.'s retreating feet, Davis turned corners and sent monstrous explosions reverberating up the stairs and down the corridors, biting enormous bits of aged and tasteful brick out of the walls, awakening guests in cold sweat, and making A.J. himself a touch nervous.

Downstairs, McGraw had finally found the freight elevator, out of three simultaneously screamed sets of directions. Fumbling with the buttons, his hands wet and slippery, feeling his gun might jump away like a bar of Dial in the shower, McGraw felt like doing nothing so much as relieving himself, in bathroom or in bed, his bowels unsettled and pins and needles in his crotch. But that wouldn't do.

He had planned to get to the sixth floor and be on the stairwell when A.J. came racing around the corner, an unsavory plan from the outset and now an unworkable one. The kid was probably on the third floor by this time. McGraw hit the sixth floor button, trying to formulate a plan, while the elevator started a tired creep up the shaft. That settled it, he was off the hook.

His only plan now was to arrive at the fifth floor in time to help Davis pick up the pieces.

Two guests who hadn't been disturbed by the

gunfire or the rolling waves of *angst* closing in the breathing space like the prelude to the storm that will end the world were Mel and Jack, sodden and unconscious in 5201, on their backs, a dresser tipped against the door, the beds being bolted to the floor. You can't figure everything.

They did not hear the final, screaming, fifth floor ricochet, did not hear a door being booted down, splitting wood, and a woman shouting her head off down the hall. Three enormous explosions, two almost at the same instant, and a great crash of erupting glass did make Jack sit up in bed, however.

He thought he was having a nightmare.

A.J. had finally torn open the door at the fifth floor, lungs ablaze and legs of jelly, and, with all he had left, smashed down the first door he came to with two hurls of his body, falling into the room and turning back to the hall. The room's occupants, already awake and terrified, man and wife, elected two opposite courses of action immediately. The woman began to shriek, unable not to, just as she was unable to take her eyes from A.J.'s profile leaning against the doorjamb, right arm extended out into the hallway. Her husband pretended to fall back asleep.

Davis had reloaded on the run, with speed that

would have won medals anywhere. He had heard
A.J.'s footsteps cease, and the wheeze of the hallway
door. He knew the kid's only hope was to kill
him—Davis was too close behind to leave any other
alternative. He was also convinced he was dealing
with a crazy, so anything was possible, and Davis
took a long moment to catch some of his breath
before spinning around the corner, dropping to one
knee, both hands extending his cannon upwards, at
that instant hearing a door breaking under lunatic
assault, the sound of screaming, and Davis was at the
top of the steps and through the door in three strides.

Davis and A.J. fired at almost the same moment,
A.J. just a hair faster, less than a dozen feet from
each other, and Davis was dead but unaware of the
fact just then. He could see a man with half a face,
blood pumping as though it were a freed prisoner
over the man's body, one mad and unseemly eye
drawing a bead on him, a mammoth handgun itself
bloodied, already raised, and Davis fired, blowing
the hallway mirror into as many shards as there are
stars, caving in a head-sized piece of wall, and scaring
hell out of everyone.

A.J. jumped across the body and headed for 5201.

McGraw had finally hit the sixth floor. Half-
dressed paying guests, stupid with sleep, ducked

hastily back into their rooms when they saw him, police special in hand, making the long run to the stairwell. He heard the shots from below, not just Davis' gun this time, and judged the gunfight to finally be underway. With any luck...

There were no further gunshots, no sound on the stairs but a woman screaming and yells from somewhere else, as though fire had broken out and was sweeping the entire floor, trapping everyone. McGraw could hear a weird thumping from the hallway as he tiptoed down the stairs, sneaked the door open, and saw Davis lying on the rug, blessedly face down, dead even to the untrained eye. The woman continued to scream. McGraw lost control of his bladder, drenching himself with a hot fountain, vision blurring and hands unsteady as his legs. Wood cracked, somewhere down the hall. McGraw peeked out.

A.J. was six doors away, smashing down the barricaded entrance to 5201 with his gun, his knees, and his entire body. The men inside were shouting, begging, and yelling snatches of prayer. In an unreal moment of his life, McGraw raised his gun, the barrel quivering as though it were held by a running engine, and tried to focus on the madman down the hall.

A.J., with no change of expression, spotted McGraw, stepped back from the door and fired four times through the woodwork, splitting the dresser and smashing a window but damaging neither of the men, who had locked themselves in the bathroom. McGraw squeezed the trigger.

The bullet whacked the metal moulding around the doorway, glanced off, and caught A.J. somewhere on the back of the skull, causing, it was diagnosed immediately afterward, massive cerebral hemorrhage and ending his stay on the planet instantly.

And that was that.

McGraw is upset, he has killed a man. He *is* normal.

Mel and Jack are under sedation.

Davis is dead, and will be missed. Peterson and his wife are dead, and will be missed. No next of kin has been tracked down to mourn the passing of the prostitute with the elusive name, as of yet. The man in the suit will soon die from the last blow of A.J.'s gun, and this will grieve many.

A.J. has left his mark.

He lies naked in a drawer, in a cold room, a tag on his toe, awaiting autopsy by interested parties.

No one is missing A.J.

The man in the glasses, overweight and un-attractive, clad in a heavy coat against the chill, has succeeded in frightening himself with the ending of a book he had vowed not to finish at work. He wishes he had honoured his own promise now, alone and spooked, a few minutes past midnight, unable to rid himself of the final, awful images from the page while he tries to concentrate on a magazine. He keeps hearing a sound from down the hall and he's trying to forget that, too.

Like a tapping.

Now if you hadn't read that damned book, he knows, you'd go straight down there and see what it was. What could it be? Nobody here but me. Hee hee.

Tap. Tap. Taptap.

Unless...rats? A rat somewhere inside...*eating?* Oh, my God, no. Very careful about that kind of thing, unthinkable, no rats. Then, what?

Tap.

I could call up. Oh yes, do that, call up and say I'm scared and I think I hear a tapping, and they say, well, what is it and I say I don't know, I'm scared to look. Get a grip on yourself and forget that book which I told you not to read anyway. Fool.

Taptaptap.

By God, that does it.

The man in the glasses stands up, frowning sternly, and strides down the high-ceilinged, institutional green corridor, lined down both sides by huge metal drawers, a cold room to be sure, and his breath precedes him. The entire room, fluorescently lit,

44

appears as a series of hallways, as though it has been divided up by giant chests of drawers.

Taptaptap. There it is, coming right from that drawer, right there. The new fellow.

Keeping his mind as blank as he can and fighting down images of huge rats dining on human flesh, the man with the glasses grasps the handle with both hands and runs the drawer out along its railing, its full seven feet, smoothly and evenly, while holding his breath.

A.J., his eyes flashing yellow, teeth clamped together in an otherworldly grin, sits straight up and kills him with a look, glasses cracking as he hits the tiles and his face turning blue before A.J. even climbs out of the drawer.

And he had arisen, and had slain his keeper, and unclothed and alone, he disappeared into the night.

II

At the Dude Ranch everything was taken care of by Lady, and there wasn't a thing to worry about —nothing at all. Pride, ambition, hope, courage: all abandoned, all in Lady's hands, the most delicious, sweetest surrender imaginable, and the most satisfying. Four acres of land in the north country, trees and clean air and Lady's house large and white in the centre of the property, the barracks at either end, and a small barn containing some essential animals: that was the Ranch.

Peace, silence, and no neighbours.

There were seven males and four females on the Ranch, and it was there that A.J. met Mona. She was chosen by Lady as A.J.'s partner during his initiation.

"I generally allow a day to acquaint a newcomer to the Ranch," Lady told him, upon his arrival. She was a tall woman, perhaps forty, with dark hair and eyes.

A.J. was standing naked in the middle of her eighteenth-century livingroom while Lady paced the floor, a willow branch in hand which she periodically ran up his cleft, or flicked him with, lightly.

"Your stay here depends on your total obedience, this is already understood," said Lady. "But of course, one must walk before one runs, musn't one?

I'm starting you with one of the females—not too much all at once—but things will proceed, they will proceed. They always do."

She hummed softly, staring blankly at some point midway between A.J. and herself.

"Now be a good boy and bend over," Lady said softly, "and then you can go to bed."

It was A.J.'s first whipping at the Ranch and the pain, while not enough to make him cry out, was aggravating—he restrained himself only barely from pulling the branch out of Lady's hand and clocking her one. But later, chained in his tiny cubicle in the barracks, lying on straw beneath a four-foot ceiling, his cock stiffened while he rubbed himself against the straw—he felt, truly, the beginning of a long, sweet surrender in which no phones were tapped, no opinions necessary, and peace was possible.

Two slaves, male, hung from the lowest branch of the huge oak, upside down, bound to the branch by their feet. The early sun beat down on them, hands tied behind their backs, faces covered by leather masks, their bodies decorated with even red stripes.

A female slave performed anilingus on a large German Shepherd dog, which the animal seemed to enjoy.

There was a slave in the outhouse, head out of

sight in the toilet bowl—male or female, it was impossible to determine through the open door.

The rest were in the barn, working on the animals, the barn wall removed so there could be no secrets.

And Lady overseeing it all.

She had Mona ride A.J. back and forth in front of the house, a bag of fishing sinkers dragging along the dirt behind him, attached to his testicles by two feet of leather cord. Two alligator clips pinched his sac under the knotted leather, two more jiggled on his nipples. He wore a bridle made for men, not horses, with a leather bit between his teeth and Mona pulling on the reins.

Lady would walk away, now and then, to oversee her other children, making small adjustments and adding new refinements, while Mona continued to ride A.J. At odd intervals Lady switched him across the ass.

Of course, there was more. Mona was also instructed to piss on him, shit on him, tie him to a tree while Lady whipped him—this time with leather thongs—and finally Lady had them tied together, face to face, and flogged them both while they rolled in the dirt.

By the end of the morning, A.J. was in love.

Freedom through pain, he thought. No thoughts of rebellion, no thoughts of revenge, no fighting the pain. Freedom. No persona to carry around and consult with on how to act, no choices possible. Only to obey. An acceptance reached through total and thorough humiliation that stripped you down to nothing, you became the recipient for everything in the world, saint-like. To reach the warm and tingling place where you know you only exist, that nothing is beyond you, you will humble yourself to anything, you are open and have no will to lose. You have lost your will. Saint-like. And at last you are no obstacle to time and space.

A.J. dragged his cock along the stiff straw, his hands chained to the wall in front of him. His body was hot and alive from the flogging before bedtime, and he knotted his muscles to bring himself as much pain as possible, his eyes watering. He felt loved.

In the seven days since his first light switching with the willow branch, A.J. had done many new things. He had tasted shit, piss, semen, been fucked up the ass repeatedly and by many, rimmed boys, sucked off dogs, and had been whipped till he cried. He had held Mona's hands while Lady whipped her, bringing her to tears, and he had become erect at the sight, envying her pain, and had been punished for it. They were paired together often, Lady even teasing them about being a young couple. A.J. did things to Mona, Mona did things to A.J., Lady did things to them both. In the meantime they shoved their tongues up whatever orifice they were directed toward and whoever or whatever it belonged to.

A.J. lay in the straw, unable to touch himself, lost in his favorite memories: the taste of Mona's feet, the feel of Mona's bare flesh straddling him, the feel of Mona's punishments, Mona sitting on his face.

Will I be ready when I leave here? Will I need nothing, be nothing, and have found peace?

A.J. lay in the straw, thinking about the taste of Mona.

"You have been a good boy, a very good boy," Lady said. "At least, most of the time. There wouldn't be much point to your being here if you had already achieved perfect obedience, would there?"

A.J. didn't answer, and certainly wasn't expected to. He stood in the middle of the livingroom, eyes straight ahead, receiving occasional love pats from Lady's willow branch.

"Mona has begun to experience something of a shift in her priorities, one could say. Since I first paired you together, an interesting thing has happened: Mona is on her way to becoming a perfect master. It is impossible to become a perfect master without having been a perfect slave, which she already is. And now you could become *her* perfect slave, being the one who triggered her switch of paths, as it were."

Lady seemed to drift away to the far past, then looked at A.J. as though seeing him for the first time.

"Why am I telling you this?" she said. "Ah, yes. I'm turning you over to Mona for the rest of the week, her alone, which is a very big first for the Ranch. At the end of the week I'm having some friends in from town, a garden party, and you'll get your chance to...graduate."

Lady smiled.

"After that, you'll be ready for the world," she said.

It is love that runs on impossible tension, a tension that sustains and is renewed hourly, impossibly. A.J. is lost in Mona's eyes, Mona in A.J.'s, as she reaches over and hurts him quickly and terrifically and he screams, lost in her face and the corners of her mouth. He lies at her feet, holding her ankles, keeping himself still for the sharp bite of the whip, hugely erect, in love.

It is the time of his time: he has surrendered.

Mona cannot stop biting him, clawing him, making him moan and bleed, riding him into the fields, spurring him, walking across his body, using him as a human toilet. No other slave on the premises, male or female, can reach Mona where A.J. can.

It is the time of Mona's time, as well.

Finally, beneath the tree in the tall damp grass, too early for bugs, after caning him in the light of dawn, she can help herself no longer. Mona straddles A.J., grabs his cock and forces it up inside herself, bouncing on her knees, and A.J. comes in fifteen seconds.

"You're going to have to get better than that," Mona tells him, pulling herself over his face. "Now suck it out."

A.J. complies.

That Saturday night, the house crowded with a dozen visitors, amidst the laughter, tinkling of glasses, and screams of agony, it is Mona who unties A.J. in the small room in back. He has been toilet slave for the entire party (with the exception of the slaves who have been eating each others' shit on stage). A.J. is drenched and dirtied, strapped in an old bathtub, and as Mona releases him, tells her,

"I'm a free man. I can do anything."

"Shut up," Mona says. "We're getting out of here."

Through the back door, across the field, along the sharp stones of the driveway she leads him, naked and reeking, to a rusted pick-up where she throws him a blanket as she turns the motor over.

And off they go.

Mona is more jealous of A.J. than vice versa, in

fact, has a touch of mania in that area. Though he could hardly be more devoted, giving, and hers alone, Mona knows what hurricanes of lust the boy can bring out, and also knows: when A.J. goes, he is gone. She wants no one else giving him the chance to go, or to set up such a distance to be reached, as she and Lady have. Mona also frets that she may never find another like him.

But A.J. seems very happy with the situation just the way it is. He cooks, cleans, makes the coffee, runs the tub, and his pupils reach saucer-like proportions when he looks into Mona's eyes.

A.J. kneels at her feet, legs apart, chin resting on her navel as he looks her in the face. Mona toes his crotch not at all gently and snaps down with the lash, covering him from shoulder blades to downy-haired ass with a burning strip of her affection.

"Is that nice, baby?" she says.

"Yes."

Mona brings down the lash.

"Isn't that nice, baby?"

"Yes."

Again.

"Oh, nice baby."

Mona lashes A.J.

"Isn't that so nice, baby?"

"Yes," A.J. tells her, eyes moist.

She lashes him.

"Oh baby, poor, poor baby," Mona whispers.

Before she lets A.J. enter her, or, more accurately,

before she puts him inside, Mona makes him masturbate twice in any one of a number of bizarre positions. Sometimes he is bent forward at the waist, a daisy sticking out of his ass, his body lipsticked with crude designs and obscene slogans. Other times he stands on the dresser near the window, legs spread far apart, the apartment in total darkness except for the flashlight beam that illuminates him for any neighbouring voyeurs, who are plentiful.

It is only after this, and after licking his semen from whatever receptacle Mona has designated, that A.J. is led into the bedroom and strapped, spread-eagled, onto the bed, held down by leather cuffs he installed himself.

A.J. can keep it up for half an hour at this point, and that suits Mona just fine.

The rest of the time A.J. stays inside, not just happy but *content*, the apartment empty of distractions, A.J. keeping house, exercising violently, and carrying himself full of Mona at all times.

A.J. is strapped to the bed, Mona running a large, soft feather over his genitals and whispering in his ear.

"Mama made lots of money tonight, baby, you know how?"

A.J. moans.

"A big, black man came up to me in the bar, the blackest man I ever saw, the colour of coal, and asked me if I knew where he and his friend could find a good time for themselves and I said, "With one little white girl?" and he thought that was funny and took me over to meet his friend who was also very large and very black."

A.J. moans.

"So we went up to their hotel, that was when I phoned from the Ritz, drank some wine and we all took our clothes off. This is a true story, honey, they gave me two hundred dollars."

A.J.'s cock is stiff and pearling. Mona beats it lightly with the feather.

"They had these *enormous* cocks, just like everyone says, and as soon as the first one had his pants off— I was already undressed— I just got on my knees and *swallowed* his cock, right down till I just had his hair rubbing against my mouth."

"Mona," A.J. breathes.

"Shh, honey, now don't be bad. I sucked on him till he was straight up like a big, black pole, then I got down and got his balls in my mouth, licked my way underneath him…"

"Ohhhh…"

"…and right around till I ran my tongue up the crack in his ass. He said no white girl had ever done that before. Then they both grabbed me—four great big huge dark hands holding me up by the ass and squeezing my tits. They turned me over on my hands and knees and one fucked me doggy-ways while one fucked my mouth. They kept changing positions and one time I got one of them fucking me right up the ass—I thought he'd just rip me apart. I was there for *hours*. One came in my cunt, one in my ass, and before I left, they both came in my mouth. Mmmm.''

"Mona," croaks A.J., "why do you hurt me this way?"

"Oh, baby," Mona purrs, "because I love you so very much, that's why. Don't you like it?"

"Yes."

"Do you really, baby?"

"Oh, yes."

"Good, that's good," Mona says, raising herself to sit on his face. "Now you give Mama a nice cleaning, it's been a long day."

The next step is to let A.J. actually *see* these wild goings-on, the descriptions of which, Mona is beginning to suspect, he only half believes. She has him bore a hole through the door of the bedroom closet, which is opposite the bed, and tack an Indian cotton bedspread over it. As long as the bedroom light is on, visibility is just fine through the thin film of material, with little chance of anyone on the other side discerning the peep-hole.

She doesn't have to clamp A.J.'s eye to the hole, she knows he won't be able to help himself.

The preparations made, she gives A.J. a light thrashing with a bamboo rod, locks him in the closet and leaves, returning some hours later with a balding, overweight tie salesman. She drags him into the bedroom, rips the clothes from her body while he is still fumbling with his belt and jumps on the bed on all fours.

Mona holds her head down near the pillow, her ass high in the air.

"Hurt me, daddy," she says. "You promised."

"Well..."

Baldy pulls off his belt, as has already been agreed upon, and gives her a tentative smack.

"Oh harder, daddy," she moans. "*Hurt* me."

He swings the belt across her wonderful, exposed ass a couple of times more, slightly harder, then actually delivers six fair-to-good whacks. Mona writhes, groaning, then leaps from the bed and drags his pants down to his ankles. She swallows the cock whole, as advertised. Before he can lose the load for good and all she pulls him onto the bed, lies on her back with her legs opened and, just as he climbs aboard, kills the lights.

For the next two minutes A.J. is treated to Mona's shrieks and heavy breathing. He can hear the thumping and mauling, but can't see a thing. Finally the salesman gives a long, shuddering sigh that is the worst sound A.J. has heard all evening.

They have a cigarette in the dark, talking in voices too low to be understood, and then light is restored.

While the man dresses, Mona languishes on the bed, caressing herself and claiming to be "too worn out to move". The salesman couldn't be happier, especially when he reaches for his wallet.

"After *that*, honey," Mona says, staring straight at the peep-hole, "consider it on the house."

A.J. watches her smile with one tear-filled eye.

Mona knows things can get out of hand at any moment, especially if she is going to go so far as letting the tricks get violent with her. One day she shows A.J. the gun.

"It's loaded, so don't fool around with it. Now, if I don't come home when I'm supposed to come home I expect you to show up right at the door with this in your hand, all right? You don't have to shoot anybody, just get me out of there. Same thing here—a trick gets out of hand, show this to him. Your face could scare a man, honey, it really could, if you felt mean."

A.J. knows that. He knows all about guns, too. Something dark is swimming toward the surface of his mind but Mona catches him, just in time.

"Now baby, I have something really special for you tonight, it's all arranged," she says in that voice that goes straight down inside him. "Let's get you strapped into bed."

She straps him face down on the bed and leaves without beating him. An hour later, with A.J. still lying on his cock, unable to think for anticipation, she returns with a friend on her arm.

"Why Bernie, *look,*" Mona cries, "there's a man in my bed!"

"What an ass!" shouts Bernie. "What an ass!"

Mona and Bernie whip off their clothes and A.J. is dry-fucked without further ado, moaning into the mattress with every plunge of the oversized cock, while Mona rims the man on top of him. Bernie comes with a wild howl.

A.J. is undone and rolled over. Bernie sits on his face while Mona lies the length of his body, his cock stiff against her belly, and sucks Bernie off while A.J. rims him. This takes somewhat longer, and Bernie comes with a quieter howl.

They take a break. Mona and Bernie chat, ignoring A.J., who serves them brandy and soda.

Bernie lies on his back while A.J. assumes the position on his hands and knees that Mona used when the tie salesman delivered the beating. His ass is high in the air, Bernie's cock down his throat. A.J. will be whipped until he makes Bernie come in his mouth. Mona lashes him sixty-three times until he swallows, at long last, the rather paltry load.

Bernie must be off, with thanks for a perfectly exquisite evening.

Mona takes a straight razor from the dresser drawer and notches A.J. above each nipple. The blood trickles down either side of his body, the streams meeting just above the navel.

"Now go to sleep, baby," Mona tells him.

A.J. stretches out on the cushions near the bed, staining them with thin lines of blood, and falls asleep almost instantly, a dark shape swimming up in his mind, to be recognized in dreams.

It is after a friend leaves his guitar behind one night after a total, drunken debauch, that Mona hears A.J. play. She is amazed to find he possesses any talents beyond the range she has plumbed, though this range is admittedly narrow.

"Why, honey, I didn't know you could do that," Mona says. "You really sound good."

A.J. puts the guitar down as quickly as he picked it up.

"Don't put it away, let me hear you."

"No," says A.J., coldly and clearly, in a voice she has never heard him use before.

"Now, baby," Mona says sternly, "don't you start saying no to me."

A.J. doesn't move to pick up the guitar, and Mona knows better than to press him on this one.

"Well, if you're going to be bad, I'll have to punish you."

"Yes."

"Let's go in the other room."

A.J. walks in and lies on the bed while Mona busies herself digging out the apparatus she'll need to teach him not to be so naughty. Curiosity still nibbles away at her.

"Did you used to play with a group, honey?"

"Sort of."

"You ever play in front of people?"

"Yes."

"Oh, really?" Mona turns, eyebrows arched. "What name?"

A.J. says nothing.

"*Baby,*" warns Mona, dragging the necessary equipment out of the drawer, "what name did you *use?*"

"Doctor Tin," A.J. whispers.

"Funny name."

Mona approaches the bed, a small smile on her lips.

"Now shall Mama teach you not to be so bad?"

"Yes. Oh, yes," A.J. whispers, rolling over.

There were funnier names going around at the time. Everything used to be possible—everything, everything.

People changed, but I didn't. Or maybe I did. You don't change anyone or anything but your own self. That's where it starts and that's where it ends.

The times were stupid, and I was stupid, but there's a way to live without playing ball and without fighting them, either. There's a way.

But there wasn't.

He knew she was dead not because she was far over her time limit, but because he felt her switch off inside him. He knew his life had changed, the same way he'd known that fact the first time he stood naked in Lady's livingroom.

—You do one thing, you try another thing, then you do something else. Nothing, on its own, touches all bases.

He pulled on the boots she'd bought him, that had never felt a city street. He wore the clothes she'd given him for those rare times they were needed.

He was as ready as he could ever be, and had totally given himself over to what he had to be. As always.

And he did go forth to seek out his enemies and to smite them; to wash his hands in their blood.

III

At one time, long before his death and resurrection—before his life, in a manner of speaking—A.J. had given almost anything a chance.

Before Doctor Tin was ever born, A.J. knew there was something wrong, very wrong, but didn't know quite what; that is to say, he was young and typical. There was a cold, burning centre he couldn't quite reach and wasn't sure he wanted to, and it was this centre that finally gave birth to, and became the nucleus of, the good Doctor.

But that was much later and not even a fantasy in A.J.'s mind the day he walked into the cool, dark office, the light slanting in through venetian blinds as A.J. settled into an over-stuffed leather chair. The lighting gave the man across the desk a light-dark-light look, a face striped and grave, with an occasional flash off his steel-rimmed glasses—A.J. suspected—for effect.

"Just say whatever comes to mind." The voice, calm, quiet and paternal, rolled across the desk.

"Everything is bullshit," A.J. said.

There was a quick, nervous giggle, then the voice found itself again.

"I'll ask you to refrain from using that kind of language," the voice said. "I'm a family man."

"Nothing means anything," A.J. said. "Life adds up to zilch."

"You are young," the voice pointed out.

"Do I have to wait till I'm fifty, to say it?"

"...and have no respect for your elders," the voice went on.

"See, that's something else," A.J. said. "Like you're supposed to respect people just because they're old. That's a hard one for me. It isn't like we live in the jungle, so surviving *means* anything—it just means growing old. That doesn't strike me as being too hard to do. Then when you're old, you eat dog food. What kind of respect is that?"

"What you have to do," the voice said, "is find a direction. You'll stop thinking about these things once you have something else to worry about."

"But the things will still exist."

"And are being dealt with by better minds than yours."

"That's just it," A.J. said. "I've got this terrible feeling that if *I* don't do something, nobody will."

"Common to your age group," the voice soothed.

"The other thing—when am I supposed to have my life?" A.J. asked. "I've been in school ever since I can remember. All the time I've been hearing, "life is wonderful, a wonderful thing", and now I'm supposed to go right from the classroom to the job. When am I supposed to have my wonderful life? Somebody told me that I've already *had* the wonderful part of my life, and I'm telling you, it wasn't so hot."

"You've been reasonably privileged," the voice said, somewhat bored. "Your life could have been much worse than it's been."

"So what?"

"I'm prescribing a mild tranquilizer for you," the voice said abruptly. "Come back and see me when you're ready to help yourself."

A.J. knew he was burning the last bridge, and hated to see it go.

"Listen, now," he said, "please listen. What's hanging me up in the worst kind of way...I just want someone to answer some questions for me, all right? What I want to know is what do you call a system where everything is a lie, the kind of lie that people even believe in when they can see with their own eyes it's not true; their whole lives are in the hands of somebody else and *that* somebody is keeping secrets from them and they think he *should* keep secrets from them; a system where we're all supposed to be stupid children, we never *do* get out of that classroom, we never have anything of our own if the hydro company decides to take it away and you can work your whole life then have the banks close on you and it's all over, anyway; a system where everyone knows and says the people running the show are crooks, *everyone* says it, and in the next breath they defend the bastards to the death. What kind of system is that?"

"Son," the voice said, shaking with passion, "you

just get a grip on yourself right this minute. That system is *democracy*."

It was the beginning of something.

As the Doctor, A.J. had been unable to spread peace, love, happiness or anything but rock 'n 'roll, which he did very well, and was the only thing that meant a fuck anyway. He went many places and lay down with many people, saw friends die, go to jail, and grow rich, and himself grew skinny on speed and crazy on psychedelics, but never lost the faith that rock was enough to let you live.

And then it was over, an LP played at 78, the needle running quickly off the final groove and suddenly the world plunged into a roaring silence.

And the violent years began.

But that was long ago, before Lady, before Mona, and long before A.J. lay in a cold drawer with his heart beating once every forty-five seconds, his mind alive with technicolour fish in deep oceans, everything overseen by an eye as large as the universe and beyond.

And now heaven did not look like such a hot place, either.

In the rooming house, A.J. receives a fifty dollar a

72

month rent deduction for acting as caretaker. Every night at eight he turns the outside light on, and once a month collects the rents. He can't get it out of his mind that even this is working for the enemy, but at this point in time it seems a small thing.

After so many large ones.

A.J. has one room with one overhead light, a hotplate and a bed. Over the bed he has a large black-and-white photograph of a woman with four men, everyone naked, the woman on her knees being taken from the rear by one man, in the mouth by another, and simultaneously jerking off the other two, one in each hand. A.J. has written under the picture, with a black felt pen: WE HAVE A MORTGAGE TO PAY.

Just to keep things straight.

The bathroom, containing both tub and toilet, is right next door and A.J. has drilled a tiny hole through the wall, appearing from the bathroom side as the memory of a removed hook. He keeps the hole blocked from his side with masking tape, making sure no light ever shows, only a hole with a dead end. At the sound of the door being closed and latched, he replaces the tape with his eye.

There are two actors, a man and a woman, living down the hall. When the woman uses the toilet she stares vacantly straight ahead, humming snatches from musicals, drumming her fingers on a bare knee, waiting for her body to finish. Undressed for the tub, still humming, sometimes singing the odd phrase in a whisper, she looks young and supple, a magazine item, but radiates absolutely nothing. If she were more banal, by merely a hair, she would be invisible.

A.J. has never jerked off thinking about this woman. He watches her faithfully, waiting for some change in that ox-brow, the gentle insinuation of a thought, any thought, but so far waits in vain.

Her partner *is* invisible. A.J. must squint, following the pattern on the wallpaper to see where it breaks, to zero in on him. He uses the toilet quickly, eyes focused on the mirror he alone can see, an inch beyond his nose. While waiting for the tub to fill he replaces his private mirror with one on the bathroom wall, his face running a wild gamut of emotional excess, muttering all the while in various pitches. Naked—like the woman—he is his own 8''x10'' glossy, a physique straight from the Y, an ad-man's idea of virility. He flexes each part of his body as he washes it, watching himself with something akin to awe.

A.J. would give a week of his life to see these two fuck. Just to cover every base.

There is a man in his early fifties, at the mercy of a government cheque, and A.J. has no idea what he does in the bathroom or how he does it. It is a base he is willing to leave bare. The man pays on time and A.J. avoids extending the conversation beyond what the day is doing outside the window.

Which also happens to be as much about the day that concerns A.J. He knows there is a time for action

74

and a time to lay low, and has suffered in his life over not knowing which times were which but now has a fair idea that, just this once, he's chosen the correct course.

He still suffers migraines from McGraw's ricochet.

There has only been one tenant who could quicken A.J.'s pulse, and she is gone now: the woman in room seven.

Her name would forever remain a mystery. She paid in cash and had the receipts made out to #7 and never wasted a word on him. Since her departure A.J. still presses his forehead to the wall, wondering at the actors, avoiding the older man, and taking in the parade of transients—seldom very interesting—but it is all reflex, now.

Whether on the toilet or in the tub, #7 filled the room in such a way that A.J. came the first time he saw her piss. Undressed, she was hardly a magazine centrefold, but A.J. could scarcely live with the vision. Unmistakeably, she owned her body and loved it. He knew what that attitude carried with it.

Sometimes, as he stroked himself slowly, to prolong the experience, staring at the lightbulb, she replaced Mona in his mind. Sometimes they were at the Dude Ranch together. Sometimes he was just lying on top of her, mouth devouring mouth, hands squeezing flesh.

She took up his thoughts asleep or awake, and it was enough to make him a contented prisoner in his tiny room, waiting for her to use the facilities next door, suffering from lover's nuts and overindulgence all at once. And when she left, he was broken.

Until he realized he'd been doing it again.

A.J. took his black felt pen and wrote, in letters six inches high, a foot above the peep-hole: DON'T JUST LIVE FOR LOVE.

He would remember.

Robert and Deedee, the actors in number three, have made the best of what they've had to work with, they feel. They have turned their room into as close a replica of a livingroom on the prairies in 1881 as is possible. Wonderful little lampshades, a chair too old to accomodate the human frame, and a marvellous table that had set them back the entire fee for a diet-Pepsi commercial give the room a delightful ambience. Covering as much of the tacky wallpaper as possible, there hang three dozen framed and faded photographs of anything, anything at all—as long as it appears sufficiently aged, faded, static and twee. Every available inch of flat horizontal surface supports a variety of pottery, carvings, pieces of driftwood, sea-shells, pretty stones, clocks that stopped keeping time forty years before, and any number of other divine discoveries. Musty bed-spreads with floral patterns reminiscent of pension-er's dresses drape dilapidated trunks, affording a sitting area complete with innumerable cushions, some emblazoned with such eye-catchers as MIAMI —HOME OF THE SUN! or embroidered with sensitive-looking horses.

Given its limitations, the room *is* divine. In fact, it reminds one somewhat of John and Arla's, Michael and Pia's, Ralph and Tony's, Fred and Peter's, Moss and Winnie's—and thirty other couples near and dear to the actors' hearts.

A.J. doesn't know any of these other people and doesn't know what to make of the place, which reminds him dimly of his grandmother who he hasn't seen since age six. He has stopped by to collect the rent and *must* sit down and have a drink, dear, we hardly know you.

A television is jammed into the corner, hopelessly updating its surroundings, and blasting out a quiz show. A jig-saw puzzle, perhaps a quarter assembled, lies on the rug in front of the set.

Robert pours him a drink, and A.J. feels as though he's just stolen third base.

"Of course," Robert says, "Deedee watches the set *constantly*, don't you, darling?"

"Shhh!"

"I have my Work," he continues, "and, as you can see, my jig-saw puzzle."

A.J. throws the drink down in a single gulp.

There are three couples on the screen, and a narrator. A partition separates each couple, who are apparently man and wife, and they all look happy, young, square and stupid. The narrator is asking a question:

"Okay, this one is for the men," he beams. "And try to be honest. Men, for ten points: my wife has farted while sitting on my face. Write yes or no."

"The fuck...?" says A.J.

"Shhh!" hisses Deedee. "Couple number one's going to win."

The studio audience, apparently gigantic, squeals and shouts while the clock chimes off the seconds, terminated by a buzzer.

"All right," the announcer begins, then laughs, begins again. "All right, ladies, for ten points we asked your husbands to answer yes or no to the question..."

"Couple number one!" shouts Deedee. "Couple number one! C'mon!"

The three women on the screen are laughing, blushing (it appears) and shaking their heads. The woman from couple #1 bets her husband would answer no, which he did, for ten points. The audience cheers frantically. Couple#1 is over the top, they can only be tied. Deedee is breathless with excitement.

The woman in Couple #2 bets her husband answered no, but he answered yes, forcing her to try and playfully slap him over the partition, yelling, "Oh you liar! You big liar!"

"Haw haw," Deedee brays, "serves you right."

The third woman, face set, bets her husband

answered yes. He answered no. She sits rigid, looking mortified.

"Yay! Yay!" shouts Deedee, then turns to A.J. "If there's two of you, you can play along with the game at home."

"Yeah," says A.J.

"My Work," Robert intones, "is first. It is my life. I am my Work. My Work is me. Piecing together an early Jackson Pollock separated into eight hundred and fifty pieces is monumentally challenging, but is not, needless to say, my Work. Ignore any deodorant commercials in which I appear—that is merely gathering shekels—it is not my Work. That dreadful T.V. production—which appears to have been shot in a rec room—in which I play the alcoholic? Dismiss it. It is not my Work. This awful stage piece with the tacky sets and me as the young son? It is not my Work. That musical last fall? It is to laugh. My Work is my life, all I live for." He throws himself on the rug beside the puzzle. "You don't mind if I tinker with this while we talk?"

"Gotta go," says A.J.

"Oh *no!*" cries Deedee, leaping to her feet. "You just *got* here. Coffee, tea, milk, mineral water, scotch, wine, freshie, grass? Like our apartment, we're going to paint it, lousy weather, how are you, nice shirt, Louise can be such a bitch. Moderation in all things, I'm okay, you're okay, there are no small parts, only small actors."

A.J. snatches up the cheque and disappears.

He has had a restless sleep. Two young boys set fire to a cat in the backyard an hour ago and the whole thing has given A.J. bad dreams. He lies sweating in the gross heat of the city, sirens interrupting people invisible to him, who seem to live their lives shouting to one another on street corners. Roaches crawl the walls unmolested, while someone vomits wretchedly into the toilet next door. A.J. can't be bothered seeing who.

His transistor radio, the size of a large package of cigarettes, buzzes the news to him from the window ledge beside the bed: how many were killed, how they died, how awful it was. The dollar is worth half a yen. Things are hopping in the major leagues, and you are all going to die—did the guy actually say that?

He turns it off. It's either news or disco—perfect music for the decade, music for a gray flannel sky, homogenized.

—How much would I get if I sold that thing?

Fifty cents. A quarter of a yen.

A television down the hall is suddenly amplified, booming through the dirty walls:

"WHAT'S THE MATTER, JACK? NO GO?"

"It's Robert! It's Robert!" Deedee screams.

"The puzzle! You're stepping on the puzzle!"

"I DON'T KNOW, FRED, I ALREADY USE AN UNDERARM FRESHENER."

A.J. is off the bed, through the door and in the hallway before he can think.

"TURN THAT FUCKING THING DOWN, YOU MINDLESS ASSHOLES!"

The volume drops below hearing range immediately. He can feel quiet shock emanating from the door.

—Well, that about does it, I guess. I'm going crazy.

A.J. lies back on the wet sheets, watching a moth beat against the light in the ceiling.

—I made my bed and now I'm lying in it. That isn't funny. Well, maybe it is funny and I've lost my sense of humour, that's a sign of being crazy, isn't it? If everything's funny, or if nothing's funny, then you're nuts.

—I could have a nice life. I could have a nice place to live, a place with a fence, and someone to live with. No more Monas. Just a nice, quiet, normal woman and a nice, normal life. I'm still young, I could learn how to do something. And we wouldn't have a radio or a T.V. or read any newspapers.

—And not talk to anyone? Or think about anything? You could get an operation to make you deaf and blind, too, you asshole.

He looks at the large scrawl across the room:
DON'T JUST LIVE FOR LOVE.
—Then live for what?

What ruined A.J.'s political development was an inability to get past the fact that the revolutionaries he met lived in large, tastefully furnished apartments that they continued to furnish, tastefully, and either drove new cars or wanted to. They were experts on the woes of East African countries and held meetings twice a week to parade their expertise.

It was not A.J.'s idea of total commitment to the oppressed peoples of the country he lived in, but then no one has ever considered A.J. particularly broad-minded.

They published an illiterate rag of a paper that could only win the hearts of the already converted and which was more embarrassing, because the issues were more real, than the *Watchtower*.

He also found the people themselves dull, unoriginal and ready to abandon thought in favour of slogans that were old and tired the moment they were hatched. They were the same kind of people he'd met in religious sects: generally not too cute, not too bright, totally inferior-feeling beings looking for something to hold onto, something that involved a group. Like the Boy Scouts.

But A.J. is apt to generalize.

He is one of six music acts appearing that night. The bass player and drummer never change from act to act. They belong to the club and they're part of the deal.

It is the first time Doctor Tin has appeared in public in some years and he has not only not been missed, he's never been heard of. He will go on first.

A talent scout for a small record company eyes the Doctor's haircut nervously in the dressing-room.

"What kind of music you play, kid?" he asks

"What kind of fucking music *is* there?" the Doctor asks.

The scout edges away, under the misapprehension that the man has just described himself as eclectic.

The Doctor knows the power of his own playing. He can tear the roof off a two-car garage and drop a heckler at thirty yards with a six-note run. He is depending on the force of his sound to halt, stupefy, and make the audience his own. Then he'll give them the message, a message they won't be able to resist.

He toys briefly with the idea of actually laying to waste the front row with a burst of sound that will smash through their chest cavities and rip out their hearts, but dismisses it as too flashy.

Doctor Tin has the message, he's seen it all, been the lamb and avenging angel, both. It has been a long road, with many detours, but he has returned —in ways and by routes the crowd will never dream of—to deliver.

When he lays down his guitar at the end of the set, it will be the beginning of a whole new game. The audience will take to the streets.

There will be change.

The Doctor's boots, out of fashion for ten years, thud across the floorboards as ominously as they've clomped across hotel lobbies not so long ago. He gives the boys on stage the time, the key, and the instruction to turn it up. His wants are simple. He plugs in his Gibson Ripper and turns to face the crowd.

The stagelights, warm and bright in his eyes, obscure the fact—momentarily—that there are twenty-three people in the place. Only four sets of eyes are directed towards him—but Doctor Tin has been in grimmer situations. He brings his heel down, hard—one, two, three times—and with one apocalyptic chord breaks into *Might As Well Be Dead*.

The effect is instantaneous and devastating. Drinks are dropped and fingers burned from forgotten cigarettes as twenty-three pairs of hands clamp tightly over forty-six ears. Some audience members actually head for the exits while others, open-mouthed, gape at the stage as though witnessing the worst car accident of their lives and at the same time discovering one of the drivers to be a dinosaur.

Doctor Tin plays, teeth grinding, trying to keep his left hand from tearing the neck off the guitar.

The bass player and drummer look at each other, lost and nervous. At the back of the club the manager tears open the door of his office, eyes bugging not so much at the volume as at the message it carries.

The Doctor has begun to sing, raw and awful, delivering the goods as straight and simple as they can be delivered. No-one can dance to it. They scream, unheeded, to TURN IT DOWN! while two bouncers fight the wall of sound and force of evil to try and reach the stage. A glass flies through the air and smashes at the insane guitarist's feet.

Doctor Tin plays.

The drummer, as distressed at not being able to follow the guitar as he is at what he's hearing, disconnects the amp, in a daring move. Five hundred watts revert to potential as silence rocks the hall, freezing the occupants in shock. But the Doctor knows his way around shock situations.

He throws the cleanest, shortest left hook he's thrown since before the Dude Ranch and gets the boot in before his man hits the floor. He is also acutely conscious of the fact, as his boot cracks a cheekbone, that he doesn't have a friend in the place.

All he wants now is to escape with his life.

A.J. was about to kick the door down to his room, when he saw there was a note stuck to it.

It read: Son the money dint come in the male I

went down they sade we are all going to be loked up in camps and I say to hell with that so I am gone.

It was from the only man in the house whose right to privacy A.J. had treated as inviolate. Inside the room, on the floor, was another note. It was a bright yellow piece of paper with a line drawing of a small girl chasing a butterfly as part of the design. Under the picture, in fountain pen, in a lovely, flowing hand was written: Sorry about the T.V. (you grumpy old bear, you!). There was a heart drawn around the message, and it was signed, The Kids down the Hall.

A.J. had a short, satisfying image of the two of them, arms and legs broken, lying in the middle of their burning room. But he had more important things on his mind.

He picked up his hotplate, dragging the plug from the socket, and began hacking at a wall, cracking the plaster and tearing it out in uneven, brittle chunks. The wall carried the largest, darkest message in the room: THE ROAD TO ACTION IS THROUGH ART.

With the hotplate falling apart in his hands, there was only one word visible to A.J.'s mad eye, the rest vanished into gaping, dusty holes: ART.

He looked at it. Then, with a final, metallic smash that tore the top right off the hotplate, it joined the rest.

McGraw was disturbed, but didn't know quite

why. A woman who'd run a farm like a nazi torture camp, two hundred miles north of the city, had had her eyes shot out that morning. The place sounded beyond belief, and it had been no cinch satisfying Doris after hearing the report. But why couldn't he sleep?

Somehow it all reminded him of the kid he'd shot, the one whose body was stolen, a case he didn't care to dwell on for a moment.

They had never identified the murdered prostitute, using only the name she rented the apartment under to give her some identity, however minimal.

They had never found out who the kid was McGraw shot, who subsequently disappeared, after causing no end of trouble.

They had never gotten a clear idea of what went on in room 1619 that evening, only that Peterson had apparently killed the woman, alone and unaided, and his two drinking buddies panicked and helped him dispose of the body.

McGraw found himself suddenly wondering about the state of health those two men were in. They had both been given suspended sentences and allowed to return to their respective cities, and as far as McGraw knew, that had been the end of it.

Except the kid's body was missing and the attendant was dead of a heart attack.

But what did it all have to do with a woman whose eyes had been shot out that morning?

Why did McGraw think it had anything to do with it?

As he finally went to sleep, McGraw decided to check on those two good old boys, in their cities far away.

And that's how he found out that Mel was dead, three days later, from being doused with gasoline and set ablaze.

A.J. had killed Lady basically for ideological reasons. She was society's outer-space tendril, maybe, but you had to start somewhere.

It had taken him a little longer to find Mel through the newspaper files, and it had cost money to reach him. But worth it.

And now Jack was back in the town where it all began. Still with the same company, which was willing to overlook character flaws in its personnel, *providing they got the job done.*

A.J. was there to do the job.

He was already in the hotel room when Jack lurched through the door, slightly drunk and beat. A flick of the light switch sobered him up, lamplight illuminating a man with a bizarre haircut sitting on a chair near the bed. The man was holding a gun.

"All I've got are charge cards," Jack said.

"Get in here and sit down."

"But I can probably scare up some cash," Jack said, moving to the bed and sitting as far away from A.J. as possible. "Or write you a cheque."

88

A.J.'s bright, magic eyes watched him.

"I don't have time to fool around with you," A.J. said, "but I wish I did. I'm the guy who was trying to break down your fucking door that night. Your friend's already dead, I set him on fire. Make you feel good?"

"I don't understand what you just said," Jack said.

A.J. was talking at the rate of three hundred words a minute, through clenched teeth.

"Forget it," he said. "I'm going to kill you. You're going to die. All right?"

Jack understood that. He jumped up and had taken two giant strides toward the door in his size eleven shoes when A.J. shot him in the back, flattening him. A.J. jumped to the body and turned it over quickly with a kick. Jack was still alive.

"What do you want?" he managed.

"You wouldn't understand," A.J. said, blowing his face in.

A.J. was not slow to leave the premises. He was flying downstairs while McGraw made the climb by elevator, the hair unaccountably standing up on the back of his arms, and the light flickering as he passed the third floor.

Two minutes later he had an A.P.B. out for "any suspicious person in the vicinity", and five minutes after that there were three blocks cordoned off around the hotel.

They were still there, engaged in a building-to-building search an hour later, when three sticks of dynamite were thrown behind the front desk of the police station, tearing the joint apart, killing six, and making a hell of a racket besides.

They arrived there too late, too.

A.J. was already away to destroy as much of their world as he could, at least a corner of it, to at least make a dent if he could not actually rend the fabric asunder.

And he did go forth in the hopes of setting an example.

Tom Walmsley is thirty years old, blond, stocky, below average height, uncircumcised, bisexual, tattooed, with bad teeth and very large feet.

In 1975, Pulp Press published his first book of poetry, *Rabies*, a documentation of Walmsley's life-long love affair with heroin and sadomasochism.

The Workingman, a one-act play, was produced by the New Play Centre that same year, and published the following spring by Pulp.

Lexington Hero was published in 1976 and is the "cleanest," most middle-of-the-road work Walmsley has ever done or ever intends to do.

Since that time, he has had *The Jones Boy* (play) produced at Toronto Free Theatre in 1977 (Pulp Press, 1978) and *Something Red* performed at the Vancouver East Cultural Centre in 1978 (New Play Centre). Tarragon Theatre will be producing *Something Red* in January, 1980, and the play will be published by Virgo Press.

Doctor Tin is Walmsley's first prose venture in ten years, and is an end to a chapter in his work. He has now said everything he has to say about sex and violence.

A CHECKLIST OF PULP BOOKS:

BOMMIE BAUMANN:
Wie Alles Anfing:
  How It All Began

LEO BURDAK:
Gearfoot Wrecks

BRIAN CARSON:
A Dream of Naked Women

TOM CONE:
Three Plays

CLAIRE CULHANE:
Barred from Prison

JANET DOLMAN & ROBERT NUNN:
Mankynde

C.W. DOLSON:
The Showplace of the County

DAN DOUGHERTY:
The National Hen

ROGER DUNSMORE:
On the Road to Sleeping Child
  Hotsprings, 2nd Edition
Laszlo Toth

KEN EISLER:
Inchman

L.L. FIELD & M.B. KNECHTEL, EDS.:
Elbow Room

RAYMOND FILIP:
Somebody Told Me I Look Like
  Everyman

D.M. FRASER:
Class Warfare

AUGUSTIN HAMON:
The Psychology of the Anarchist

CARL HARP:
Love and Rage

ALFRED JARRY:
Ubu Rex (Translated by David Copelin)

CHRIS JOHNSON:
Duet for a Schizophrenic

MARY BETH KNECHTEL:
The Goldfish that Exploded

JOHN KULA:
The Epic of Gilgamesh as
  Commissioned by Morgan

BETTY LAMBERT:
Crossings

MARK MADOFF:
Paper Nautilus
The Patient Renfield
Dry Point

CARLOS MARIGHELLA:
Minimanual of the Urban Guerilla

MARK MEALING:
Coyote's Running Here

ROMAINE MURPHY:
The Molly Bloom Poems

ROGER PRENTICE & JOHN KIRK:
A Fist and the Letter

NORBERT RUEBSAAT:
Cordillera

BRIAN SHEIN:
Theatrical Exhibitions

JOHNNY TENS:
Tenth Avenue Bike Race

CHARLES TIDLER:
Whetstone Almanac
FLIGHT: The Last American Poem
Anonymous Stone

TOM WALMSLEY:
Rabies
The Workingman
Lexington Hero
The Jones Boy
Doctor Tin

ANTHONY WILDEN:
The Imaginary Canadian

MARK YOUNG:
Brother Ignatius of Mary

PLEASE WRITE:
Pulp Press
Box 3868 M.P.O.
Vancouver, Canada V6B 3Z3
FOR A DESCRIPTIVE CATALOGUE.